Pal the Pony
Pal and Sal's New Friend

by R. A. Herman
illustrated by Betina Ogden

SCHOLASTIC INC.
New York   Toronto   London   Auckland   Sydney
Mexico City   New Delhi   Hong Kong   Buenos Aires

For Simone, who hasn't been on a horse yet.
— R.A.H.

For Paris
— B.O.

ISBN 0-439-68119-7

Text copyright © 2005 by R. A. Herman.
Illustrations copyright © 2005 by Betina Ogden.
All rights reserved. Published by Scholastic Inc.
SCHOLASTIC and associated logos are trademarks
and/or registered trademarks of Scholastic Inc.

12 11 10 9 8 7 6 5 4 3 2   5 6 7 8 9 10/0

Printed in the U.S.A.
First printing, February 2005

Pal and Sal have a new friend.

His name is Hal.

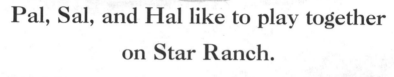

Pal, Sal, and Hal like to play together
on Star Ranch.
In the summer, they swim in the pond.

In the fall, they roll in the leaves.

In the winter, they play in the snow.

Now it is spring.
Pal, Sal, and Hal run in the fields.

They smell the flowers.

Pal and Sal nibble the grass and swish their tails.

Nibble, nibble. Swish, swish.

Hal tries to catch the flies.

Hal rolls in the mud.
Pal and Sal roll in the mud, too.

The cool mud feels good.
Squish, squish, squish.

Then Pal, Sal, and Hal play tag.
"I'm hungry," barks Hal.

"Let's go back to the ranch for dinner."
Pal, Sal, and Hal race back to the barn.

"You are so dirty," says Kate.

"You all need a bath!" says Billy.

Billy gets the hose.

Kate gets the brushes and tub.

Pal and Sal get a bath.

"Come on, Hal.
Time for your bath," calls Billy.

But Hal is not there.

They all look for Hal.
They look in the barn.

They look in the corral.
But no one can find Hal.

Pal runs into the fields.

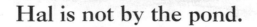

Hal is not by the pond.

Hal is not in the mud.
Pal cannot find Hal anywhere.

It is getting dark.

Pal is worried.

Then he hears a cry.
The sound is coming from the well.

Pal sees Hal inside the well.
"I did not want a bath," says Hal.

"So I ran away. But I fell into the well.
I cannot get out!" says Hal.
Pal has a plan.

He runs back to the barn.

He grabs a rope.
Sal follows Pal.

Pal throws the rope into the well.
Hal grabs the rope with his teeth.

Pal and Sal pull the rope.
They pull and pull.
They save Hal!

Hal is glad to be out of the well.

He runs in circles.

He wags his tail.

He jumps up and licks Pal and Sal on the nose.

They all go back to the ranch.
Hal has a bath!